P9-CBF-502

Lone Star

The ONCE UPON AMERICA® Series

Lone Star

A STORY OF THE TEXAS RANGERS

BY KATHLEEN V. KUDLINSKI

ILLUSTRATED BY RONALD HIMLER

VIKING

Many thanks to Tom Burks, historian at the Texas Ranger Hall of Fame and Museum in Waco, Texas, and Kathleen J. Hoyt, historian at Colt's Manufacturing Company, who read this text for background authenticity.

VIKING
Published by the Penguin Group
Penguin Books USA Inc., 375 Hudson Street, New York, New York 10014, U.S.A.
Penguin Books Ltd, 27 Wrights Lane, London W8 5TZ, England
Penguin Books Australia Ltd, Ringwood, Victoria, Australia
Penguin Books Canada Ltd, 10 Alcorn Avenue, Toronto, Ontario, Canada M4V 3B2
Penguin Books (N.Z.) Ltd, 182–190 Wairau Road, Auckland 10, New Zealand

Penguin Books Ltd, Registered Offices: Harmondsworth, Middlesex, England

First published in 1994 by Viking, a division of Penguin Books USA Inc.

1 3 5 7 9 10 8 6 4 2

Text copyright © Kathleen V. Kudlinski, 1994
Illustrations copyright © Ronald Himler, 1994
All rights reserved

LIBRARY OF CONGRESS CATALOGING-IN-PUBLICATION DATA
Kudlinski, Kathleen V. Lone star: a story of the Texas Rangers /
by Kathleen V. Kudlinski; illustrated by Ronald Himler. p. cm.
Summary: In 1847, eleven-year-old Clay dreams of becoming a Texas Ranger
so that he can exact revenge upon the Comanche Indians who attacked
his family, until personal experience acquaints him with the
brutal reality of Ranger activities.
ISBN 0-670-85179-5
[1. Texas Rangers—Fiction. 2. Texas—Fiction.] I. Himler,
Ronald, ill. II. Title.
PZ7.K9486Lo 1994 [Fic]—dc20 93-23048 CIP AC

ONCE UPON AMERICA® is a registered trademark of Viking Penguin,
a division of Penguin Books USA Inc.
Printed in the U.S.A.
Set in 12 pt. Goudy Oldstyle

For Barb, very dearest friend

Contents

Broken Glass

"Oww! Oh, Clayton, make it stop hurting."

Clay swallowed hard and held Betsy's leg even tighter. Her foot looked tiny and pale against the doctor's black leather table. Tiny and pale and bloody.

"You don't have to look if you don't want to," Doc Williams said. He unwrapped Betsy's bandage from her foot. She screamed and tried to pull free. "Just hold your little sister still."

Clay looked away. His eyes went to the bloodstains on Betsy's pinafore, and looked away. He glanced at the wanted posters on the wall. Some were from two years ago, 1845. There were some pictures of Comanche warriors, too.

A bad taste filled Clay's mouth. Were they the ones who'd attacked his family? He gritted his teeth. The shiny metal tools in a basket on the doctor's table caught his eye. Scissors and pliers, a saw and needles.

"No, no, no, no, no!" Betsy yelled. Clay looked at Doc Williams. Gray hair hung over the doctor's forehead as he studied Betsy's cut. How can he be so calm? Clay wondered. And Doc's face wasn't just calm. He seemed, Clay thought, fascinated by the wound.

For the first time, Clay looked right into the mess. His breath stopped. The cut wasn't bleeding so much now, so he could see inside—inside a real foot! Sliced open that way, the skin looked thick, like cowhide. Inside was all glisteny and smooth. And there was bright red muscle, too, and white, waxy bubbles just under the skin.

"What are those?" he couldn't help but ask the doctor.

"Fat. And those are tendons." Doc Williams used the end of his tweezers to point to some white stringy pieces. Clay leaned closer. Betsy whimpered, and he patted her knee without thinking.

"Now, those tendons"—Doc tilted Betsy's foot a bit so Clay could see—"those hook your sister's toes to muscles up in her calf. That layer there wraps around the bones."

Clay wiggled his toes inside one boot. He tried to feel all those parts in his own foot. The doctor grabbed a piece of glass from deep inside a muscle and pulled.

"Oooh, stop," Betsy begged. Suddenly Clay remembered that this was a real, live foot. A blast of dizziness made him step backward.

"Steady there, Clayton," Doc Williams said. He held the scrap of brown glass out to show Betsy.

"There're a few more of these in there, honey. You'll have to be brave. These are from a Dr. Jake's patent medicine bottle, aren't they?" Betsy nodded. Her face was white.

"That's why I had to carry Betsy here," Clay said in a rush. "Mama took her morning dose of Dr. Jake's. It always makes her act strange. Mostly she falls asleep."

Doc Williams looked up from Betsy's foot. "Your mama taking the dose right often now?"

"Before every meal, unless her hands are paining her bad." Doc Williams seemed to be waiting, so Clay went on. "The pain comes pretty often, now. And the doses." He pictured his mother taking a "dose." She still took the silver spoon out of the drawer, but she didn't use it anymore. She'd just pull the stopper out and drink the strong syrup right down. Sometimes she drank a whole bottle. Sometimes two.

"What's Dr. Jake's made of?" Clay wondered out loud.

"It's just like whiskey," Doc said, "with something a little stronger thrown in."

Clay nodded. This must have been a two-bottle morning, he figured. He'd come running from the shed when he heard Betsy scream. There was broken bottle glass all

4

over the kitchen floor. He remembered seeing a shiny spoon sitting on the counter. He hadn't bothered to look for Mama. She'd be in the bedroom, her poor hands tucked into the pillow under her head.

He shook his head. "That's why I've *got* to be a Texas Ranger, Doc. Eleven is too young, but as soon as I can pass for 18 or so I'll go down and sign up. I'll find my brother and I'll get those Comanches back for what they did to us." He paused until he could trust his voice again. "It's all I ever think about."

Betsy and Doc Williams were both staring at him. Clay realized he'd been shouting. Then he realized what he'd shouted.

"It was before we came to town, Betsy. You were still a baby. Doc took care of Mama. We weren't going to tell you." Clay looked to Doc Williams for help.

"Let's get back to that foot, young lady." The doctor said, "Clay, hold her." Betsy screamed and sobbed as Doc Williams pulled slivers of glass from the cut. Clay wanted to run out into the street to get away from the sound, but Doc didn't even seem to hear it.

"Can't you make it stop hurting?" Clay begged, finally.

"Son, I wish I could. There's nothing anybody can do for pain. Maybe someday . . ." Doc trailed off. "For now, we just have to operate like this; fix it right and quick as we can. Hold her."

"I'll give her some of Mama's syrup as soon as I get her home."

5

"No, you won't!" Doc Williams shouted. Betsy went silent and white. "You see what it has done to your mother, Clayton? And she's not the only one who just can't get enough Dr. Jake's. I'll never tell anyone to use that gosh darn syrup again. Never."

Betsy stayed silent while Doc finished working.

So did Clay.

Sweet on Seth

"Shush, now, Betsy." Clay put his sister down onto the settee. He stood up and stretched his back. "Hoo-eee, but aren't you getting big?" She hadn't seemed so heavy when he'd picked her up—all tears and screams—to carry her to Doc's office. And she had seemed only a little heavier when he'd begun the trip home. Clay had pretended to be a Texas Ranger rescuing a child stolen by the Comanches.

"I'll see if Mama is awake yet," he said, putting Betsy's foot up on a pillow.

"I'm thirsty!" she answered. "And my foot hurts."

"Mighty pleased to meet you, Miss Thirsty," Clay said.

"I'm Thirstier Still!" The sound of Betsy's laughter followed him into the kitchen.

"Caroline!" Clay stopped in surprise. "What are you doing home from school?"

Clay's older sister turned quickly from the dry sink. "I sent the children home early." She pushed a broom at him. "Quick, I need to clean up. Seth is coming for supper"—she reached up to smooth a loose hair—"and Mama is, well . . ."

Clay took the broom handle and started sweeping. "Slow down," he said. "Who's Seth?"

"He's new in town." Caroline's voice was getting faster. "He could live anywhere he wants, but he says he might stay here a while, now that he's met me."

"Well, la-di-da!"

"Don't tease, Clay. I need your help. There's all this mess on the floor. And supper to make. The table to set. Mama is still resting. I have to braid Betsy's hair. And I want to put on my Sunday dress, too." Caroline pulled at her apron. "Oh, where do I start?"

Clay looked at his sister in astonishment. What had her so skittery? She'd been putting food on the table three times a day since they'd come to town. Since the Indian attack. Caroline's face looked flushed and her eyes were sparkly bright. "You feeling poorly?" he started to ask, then stopped.

"Why, you're getting sweet on Seth!" Clay's mind spun like a dust devil on a hot afternoon. If she got really sweet on somebody, Caroline might get married. He pushed the broom across the floor. If she got married, she would leave. He swept harder. What would happen then?

Who would cook when Mama had taken her medicine? Who would get clothes? He pushed the broken glass into a corner of the floor. Who would take care of Betsy? He stamped out the door with the dustpan, and threw the glass on the dump beside the shed. The pieces glittered in the hot July sun. Who would take care of *him* if Caroline left?

"Seth can't come to supper!" he announced as he stepped back inside. "I won't let him."

"Oh, Clay." Caroline grinned at him. "You're such a tease!" She hummed and patted out some biscuit dough. Clay stared at her back until she put the biscuits into the cookstove and turned around. She looked at his face. "You're not fooling, are you?"

He slowly shook his head no.

"Why ever shouldn't Seth come? You don't even know him." Clay kept shaking his head. "Well, you'll see why I've taken a liking to him when he gets here. He is handsome and tall and strong. And he has the most wonderful smile . . ."

Clay slammed plates onto the table. It was worse than he thought.

"Clay, he's funny, too, like you." Clay looked at her. She had flour on her cheek where she'd pushed her hair up again. He wanted to brush the flour off his sister's face—but he wanted to shake her, too. How *could* she think about leaving?

"Caroline . . ." he began, but his voice wouldn't say more.

"Why, Clayton, I do believe you're jealous!" Caroline laughed gaily and threw her arms around Clay. "I do love you, baby brother," she said.

Clay stood stiff with shock. Had she forgotten all about Clem? Clement John Andrews? The *real* baby of the family? Clem could be somewhere with the Comanches right now! He remembered the feel of the tiny boy in his arms. When I'm a Ranger, he thought, I'll find him. We'll all be back together again. He squeezed Caroline as tight as he could.

She laughed again. "There, see now, everything is right as rain."

"Clayton, Caroline? What time is it?" Mama leaned against the kitchen doorway. Clay wished she would comb her hair sometime.

Clay looked at Caroline. There was flour all over her face now, and her hair was ruffled, but she still looked pretty.

"I'm still thirsty!" Betsy wailed from the front room.

And there was a knock at the back door. A man's voice called, "Caroline? Am I too early to sit a while with you before supper?"

Caroline screamed and ran out of the kitchen. Mama staggered back into the bedroom, and a tall stranger

10

stepped in through the back door. "Begging your pardon," he said, "but have I found the right house?"

Clay's mouth opened, then closed, then opened again. This had to be Seth. He was tall like Caroline had said, and his grin was as wide as it was bright. He was dressed like a regular cowpoke, except that his brown hair and mustache were slicked into place. But all Clay could stare at were the guns.

There were two big revolvers tucked into his belt. Clay had seen a third tucked into the back when the man had closed the kitchen door. A fourth hung in some sort of sack from his right hip and a powder horn dangled from a strap around his neck. A sheath knife hung from his left hip and another peeked from the top of his boot.

Who was this man? No uniform, so he wasn't a soldier. No badge: he wasn't a lawman. Caroline said he was new in town. Free to go anywhere. Clay started to smile.

"She never told me you are a Texas Ranger!"

Cooking a Spotted Pup

"Did you kill any Comanches?" It spilled out before Clay could stop it. "That's what I'm bound to do. I'm going to get them for what they did to us. Did you get any? Did you?"

"Whoa there, partner. We haven't even been introduced. You are . . ."

"Clayton Andrews." Clay stood straighter as he said his name. Why had he let himself sound like such a child?

"I'm Seth Brown." The Ranger sniffed the air, then opened the cookstove door. "I'm willing to sit down and jaw for a month with you, but first we've got to rescue these biscuits."

Clay gave Seth a pot holder. "You cook?" Clay asked. "But you're a Ranger!"

"I've worked as a cowhand on and off since I first signed up to fight against General Santa Anna in Mexico," Seth said. "I wasn't much older than you back then." He grinned. "When you're about to starve, you learn to hunt real quick—and then to cook whatever you bring in."

Clay looked up at Seth. He had to be six feet tall. There wasn't anybody in town this big. His chest looked to be a mile across and his thighs seemed as thick and hard as tree trunks. "Well, you surely did not starve!" Clay said. They both laughed at that.

Seth moved an iron skillet to the top of the stove. "This beef's for supper?" He pointed to the meat lying on the wooden counter.

"I guess so," Clay said.

"You know how to fry up a tough old steak like this one?" Clay shook his head no. "Get me a handful of flour and a pepper grinder. We'll have this done before Caroline comes out of hiding." The Ranger winked at Clay.

When Caroline finally carried Betsy in, a piece of salt pork was already dancing in its grease in the skillet. Clay was patting flour and pepper into the steak. "Don't be so gentle," Seth was telling him. "You've got to pound all the tough right out of that mean old longhorn. Show it who's boss with the butt end of this knife."

"Hello, Seth," Caroline said. Her voice sounded softer than Clay had ever heard it. Betsy looked surprised too.

"You got some rice and raisins?" was Seth's only answer to her. "Clay and I will boil them together and cook up a spotted pup for dessert. Maybe we'll sweeten it with molasses if you've got a lick of that about."

"Now wait a minute." Caroline's voice wasn't so soft now. "*I'm* supposed to be fixing *you* a supper."

"Shush, girl, and sit down a bit. Like we say out on the range, 'Only a fool argues with a skunk, a mule, or a cook.' "

"And which are you?" Mama stood at the doorway. Her hair was combed, her dress was neater, and her eyes were almost clear.

Clay smiled. They hardly ever saw her this lively anymore.

"Oh, Mama." Caroline jumped to her feet and led her mother to the chair. "This is Seth. I told you all about him."

"Not quite."

"Mama, Mama!" Betsy wailed suddenly. "I cut my foot."

"Show me." Mrs. Andrews guided Betsy down onto her lap. "Did Caroline put this bandage on?"

"Doc Williams did. And Clay carried me all the way there and all the way back again. Then Caro brushed all my hairs out. And nobody, *nobody* will get me a drink."

"I must have been, ah, sleeping," Mrs. Andrews said.

Seth dropped the steak into the skillet and the kitchen filled with a loud sizzle and the rich smell of frying meat. "I'll need some milk for the gravy," he said. "And you

might get some extra milk for that helpless, hairless princess on her throne there."

"I am *not* helpless!" Betsy slid off Mama's lap and hopped around on one foot. "See? And I have beautiful braids." She pulled them out sideways to prove it to Seth. "Caro even said so!"

In the laughter that followed, Clay went out to the shed to fetch a bowlful of milk. When he got back, Caroline and Seth were working side by side at the stove. They looked nice that way, he thought. And hadn't Caroline said that Seth might just stay around here?

Everyone was still laughing as supper was put on the table. Seth had one story after another to tell about the life of a cowboy.

"Texans aren't the first cowboys," he said. "Though, of course, we're the best. The first cowboys lived way up in New England 70 years ago. They didn't ride horses or rope cows. No sir, they were called cowboys because they wore cowbells!"

"Why ever?" Caroline asked. She leaned close to Seth, Clay noticed, and kept him talking on and on. Clay didn't mind the talking part.

"The cowboys liked being part of merry old England. To help the British redcoats, they hid in thickets and pretended to be lost cows." Seth mooed long and loud, and Betsy clapped her hands and laughed.

"When a colonist came into the thicket looking for the poor cow, the 'cowboy' would shoot him, dead. There'd be one less soldier to fight against good King George."

Mama sighed and closed her eyes. Clay thought her hands must be hurting.

"Tell one about the Rangers," Clay asked.

"I'll be happy to. Fact is, if you'll keep passing the food this way, partner, I'll talk the ears right off your head." Clay took extra helpings too.

"You know about Bigfoot and the black bean?" Seth asked.

Clay nodded. Everyone knew that story. He wanted to hear about the settlers that Seth had saved or the horse thieves he had caught. Or best of all, the Comanche warriors he had killed.

"Bigfoot! I want to hear about Bigfoot!" Betsy cried.

"Well," Seth began, "old Bigfoot Wallace is a foot taller and three feet wider than me."

"Really." The way Mama said it, it wasn't a question.

"That's the way I remember him, ma'am, but you know how things can grow a bit once they're planted in a mind." Mama tightened her lips. "Well, Bigfoot and a passel of other Rangers were having a fine old time down in Mexico, just to show that rascal Santa Anna what Texas men are all about. Their captain was hurt and he surrendered to the Mexican troops. They had to walk 300 miles through the desert to a jail at Hacienda Salado. They were hungry and tired and thirsty."

"I hate to be thirsty," Betsy said.

"Bigfoot Wallace helped others escape from the jail, but the Mexicans caught them all and said that they would shoot one tenth of the Texans as a punishment.

The Mexicans filled a pot with beans; 176 white ones and 17 black ones. Each prisoner had to put his hands in and pull out a bean. Those who got white beans could live—"

"Did Bigfoot get a black one?" Betsy asked.

"No. He got a white one, but he offered to trade it with anyone who got a black bean."

"Did anyone trade?"

"No. And to this day, Rangers have never surrendered again. After what happened in Mexico, they never will. They never give up their guns. They never take prisoners. They never fire the first shot. And, like old Bigfoot, they are always ready to die for a fellow Ranger."

Clay's head rang with the sound of drumming horses' hooves and gunfire. How could anyone who fought with the Rangers' rules ever lose? He couldn't wait to join up.

"Sounds a lot like the Comanches, themselves," Mama said. Caroline gasped and there was a sudden silence around the table.

"Is that story true?" Betsy asked.

"Well, some say it is true and some say it's a bit of a tall tale. But Bigfoot Wallace is real." Seth grinned. "He wiggled his way back out of Mexico, and he and Jack Hays are ready to go fight General Santa Anna again. The only thing is, this time Bigfoot and the Rangers won't be fighting for the Republic of Texas. We'll all be fighting for the United States."

"I just loved New Year's Day last year," Caroline breathed. "Remember waking up to 1846 and suddenly being United States citizens?" Her voice shook. "A new flag, a new president, a whole new start." Betsy clapped and Seth grabbed Caroline's hand in the excitement.

Clay had a sudden, terrible thought. "Will the United States keep the Texas Rangers?"

"There will always be Texas Rangers," Seth said. He was still holding Caroline's hand, Clay noticed. "We will fight to keep Texans safe, from Indians, from Mexicans, from cow thieves and robbers . . . fighting wherever we're needed."

"How do I sign up?" Clay asked. "I'm ready now!"

"You report in with a good horse. They want it to be worth 100 dollars, or more."

"Why?" Caroline asked.

"A Ranger is only as good as his horse. If you're patrolling 1,000 miles or more a month, you want a good horse and"—Seth winked at Clay—"a mighty comfortable saddle."

"I've got that already." Clay pictured himself riding Diamond across the Texas prairie. "What else do I need?"

"You have to have 100 rounds of ammunition and a good gun. You don't happen to have those, too, do you?"

"I have Pa's horse and saddle. I have his ammunition and his gun. I want to join!"

Clay would have gone that instant, but Caroline whispered to Seth, "He's not a very good shot."

Clay's shoulders fell. If you had to be a great shot, he could never join up. "Who's been teaching him?" Seth demanded.

20

Caroline looked up into his eyes. "There hasn't been anyone since Papa . . ."

"Well, I could show him . . ."

"Oh, would you?"

Caroline threw her arms around Seth's neck.

"I think I need some of my medicine," Mama said.

Seth turned to Clay. "Meet me tomorrow early where the creek runs into the Brazos River. And bring that old gun of yours."

"Yep." It didn't matter how it had come about. Clay was going to learn how to shoot. And with a real Ranger!

Longhorn

"Mama, before you take your medicine, can I go down to the creek?" Clay asked.

Seth and Caroline had gone to the pump to fetch water to wash the dishes. Betsy was taking a nap.

"Why, Clayton, you haven't asked to go to the stream since, well, since we came to town," Mrs. Andrews said.

"I'll be back in time to milk Esther, I promise."

"Well, if you're not, I'll have Caroline do it. Or maybe this all-purpose Rangerman will take over that job, too." As Clay turned to go, he saw her take out the spoon.

Go easy, Mama, he wanted to say, but he knew she wouldn't listen to him. He hurried out the door.

They'd all tried, from Caroline saying she'd call the sheriff to little Betsy begging, "Please, please, don't drink that, Mama." Betsy was the only one who ever bothered anymore. Clay thought about what Betsy sounded like: so hopeful and so hopeless.

He felt the white-hot hate coiling like a rattlesnake in his gut, ready to strike. Wait till I'm a Ranger, he said to himself. I'll get the Comanches who did this to us. Slowly the hate snake uncoiled, Clay's muscles relaxed, and his breathing came easy again.

He hurried to the shed and put the saddle on Diamond. "Hey, friend, you haven't been ridden enough," he said. He tried to pull the cinch belt up tight. He smacked the horse's belly. Diamond let out the breath he'd been holding but the cinch still wouldn't buckle in its old spot. "You're fatter than a barrel!"

"I know how to fix that," he promised, as he swung into the saddle. "A thousand miles a month should about do it." He needed a good horse, Seth had said. Well, this was one fine cayuse. He tightened his knees and Diamond took off, cantering easily over the low grass-covered hills toward the line of trees beyond. Cantering on Diamond was like sitting in a rocking chair, Clay thought. He could be happy doing this for years.

Clay eased Diamond around clumps of prickly pear and thorny mesquite, by laying the reins across one side of the horse's neck or the other. He reached forward and rubbed Diamond's neck.

Tonight he'd clean his father's gun. "Bring along that

old gun of yours," Seth had said. Just wait until he saw what kind of gun Clay had! It wasn't just your everyday single-shot pistol. No sir, Papa had gotten one of those newfangled revolvers to protect his family.

Clay swallowed quickly at that thought and tried to remember exactly how many balls were left in the ammunition sack. Did he have enough gunpowder? And had the primer caps stayed dry in their tin? He hoped there was enough of everything.

If he needed more, he supposed he could spend some of the money he was earning at the blacksmith's shop. He'd always given the money to Mama. Now he wondered if any of it was left. For all he knew, it might all have gone to the traveling peddler who sold Dr. Jake's patent medicine. It was an awful thought. Clay squeezed Diamond into a full gallop.

He pulled up to a walk to go over the steep bank. Here the stream had washed away a little gully. Down in the wash, the air was cool. Live oaks and cottonwoods shaded the ground. A mockingbird sang on and on, making up the tune as he went along. Clay listened and squinted into the trees, trying to find it.

Suddenly the bird flushed into the air from a pecan tree. Its wings and tail flashed gray-white-gray. A road-runner bolted from the brush, and a flock of quail exploded in a dozen different directions.

Clay sat tall on Diamond, trying to see what had spooked the birds. It was the MacMurtry boys and their friends, naked as newborns.

"Don't suppose you'd want to go swimming with us," said Robert, the oldest MacMurtry. Clay shook his head no. These were the town's troublemakers. The younger ones had all made Caroline angry, at school. The older ones hadn't seen the school for years.

"Nah, that goody-goody would probably rather go to school with his sister than swim with the boys," teased a younger MacMurtry. Clay turned Diamond and walked silently beyond the bend in the stream.

The boy didn't deserve an answer. Besides, he was right. There was much, much more Clay wanted to know about. And running with a pack of boys had never looked good to him—especially boys like the MacMurtry gang.

He thought about the Texas Rangers. They were loners too. Mostly they patrolled alone or in pairs. They attacked like lightning and left just as fast. Never taking prisoners. Never surrendering. Never firing the first shot. Clay wished he'd brought his father's gun along to practice with today. *His* gun, Clay corrected himself. It was his own gun now.

Why couldn't he learn to shoot it like his papa had? It didn't seem to matter how much target practice he did, he just couldn't shoot straight. Maybe Seth could help. Clay hoped so.

Diamond's hooves splashed as they walked upstream. Clay looked at the drifts of broken branches and dead grass caught at saddle height in the tree trunks. There'd been some heavy thunderstorms this summer. The Indians called them "male storms," heavy and fast and exciting. The flash floods that followed had been deeper than Clay was tall. He looked at the steep banks of the wash. Could he have scrambled out in time? He was not sure.

"Female storms," the soft gentle rains of the winter and spring, never left scars like this, he thought. They left new green leaves and fields of bluebonnets, instead. The fields of blue were long gone, now, and thunderheads gathered almost daily over the mountains.

Diamond shifted under him. "Whoa, boy," Clay said. He looked where the horse's ears pointed. Nothing. Diamond blew nervously. A big rattler? Clay wondered. A wild hog? The MacMurtrys playing tricks? Diamond whickered and took several steps backward. Could it be Indians? They sometimes raided this close to town. Clay swallowed hard. Why hadn't he brought Pa's gun?

Diamond sidestepped and froze. There, in the stream, stood a big old longhorn bull. The animal stood as wide as Diamond and almost as tall. His hide was black and white and gray and brown all melted together. His wide horns were ivory white, curved and sharp—and they were lowered toward Diamond.

Clay had been told about wild bulls. About how you couldn't trust one when it had claimed a territory. How sometimes they'd let you pass just as polite as you please. How sometimes they'd bluster and fuss and finally back down. And how sometimes they'd kill anything that came onto their turf. They gored with those horns and stomped with those hooves until there wasn't much left but a smear and a prayer.

The bull shook his head at Clay and stamped in the creek. The points of his horns ripped branches from the trees. His wattles swung from side to side. The bull turned to look upstream and snorted, then swung his big head back. He was glaring at Diamond, but his ears kept flicking back to listen.

What could be up there? The bull shifted and snorted again, and lowered his head. Clay held his breath. Suddenly the longhorn wheeled, and splashed upstream. He went crashing into the bushes.

"Aie-yeee!" someone yelled in terror. A child screamed. Clay pulled Diamond around and charged downstream, away from the bull. From the screams. He dug his heels into the horse's side at the first chance to climb the steep bank. Diamond heaved and snorted and scrambled up in the soft dirt.

Clay urged him to gallop without looking back. His mind was filled with the sound of those screams and the pictures they called from his memory. Memories of old screams. Of dashing up out of a wash years ago. Of finding his father, shot through with arrows and scalped. Finding Caroline whimpering in the well. Finding Betsy in the big chest with Mama, and Mama's fingers all broken where the lid had been slammed on them to save her.

And no sign of little Clem anywhere, anywhere.

Rattlesnake
Justice

"Sun's up, Clayton!" Caroline's voice sang to him from the kitchen. "Time's a-wasting and Esther needs to be milked."

Clay groaned and threw the sweaty sheets to the floor. What was Caroline so happy about? He was still buttoning up his pants when he stumbled into the kitchen.

"My, but you're a sight," Caroline scolded. "Go put a shirt on!" Clay looked down at the tops of his long johns. They were only a little gray around the cuffs. Except for a splash of dried gravy on his chest, they were clean. Almost. "What's wrong with this?" he asked. "I've only worn it a week."

It wasn't fair for her to be picking on him, he thought. Not after he'd spent the whole night remembering old nightmares and dreaming new ones.

"Get yourself dressed and milk the cow, Clay. Seth will be here any minute to go shooting with you."

Suddenly the night—and the nightmares—didn't matter. "Wait till Seth sees Pa's gun!" he called, as he changed his clothes. He dug the revolver out of the bottom of the chest where it lay, safe in its own box. Clay looked at the five-shooter silently for a moment before tucking it into his belt. Then he looped the loading lever and powder horn around his neck and grabbed the ammunition sack. He headed out to the shed.

"Morning, Esther," he said, as he pulled the milking stool close. The cow gave a low moo. "Sorry I'm late." He reached for her udder, and his powder horn banged into her side. Esther kicked and knocked over the milk bucket and Clay fell backward.

He was picking straw out of the bucket when Doc Williams came through the shed door. The doctor looked at the gun, the pouch, and the powder horn. "You and Esther expecting an ambush this morning?"

"You never know, Doc. These are dangerous times." The doctor laughed and offered his hand to help Clay to his feet.

"I stopped by to see how Miss Betsy is doing," he explained. "And to say you did a powerful good job with her yesterday."

"I just did what anybody would," Clay said, and bent more carefully to start milking.

"Not everybody can look into a wound and see beyond the blood. You did, didn't you?" Clay nodded silently as the milk started hissing into the bucket. He remembered the glistening beauty of all the parts inside Betsy's foot. He looked at his hand pulling on Esther's udder. A hand would have even more inside, he figured.

"You didn't scream or faint or run, either," Doc said.

"I wanted to."

"But you didn't, did you? Clay, are you dead set on becoming a Texas Ranger?"

"Sure he is!" Seth's voice boomed through the little shed. Esther kicked in surprise, but Clay had grabbed the milk bucket in time. He looked up to see the two men staring at each other.

"Doc Williams, this is Seth Brown. He's a Texas Ranger."

"So I see. One of Jack Hays's boys. You on a patrol through here, Mr. Brown?"

"Just for a few more days. Then I'm off to Mexico."

"But I thought . . ." Clay began.

"I'm the only doctor in these parts, Mr. Brown," Doc said. "I expect our trails will cross. Fires, floods, snakes, and Rangers keep me busy."

"Well, Doc, I suppose that's so." Seth grinned and tipped his hat at the doctor. He stepped back out into the hot morning sun. "When you're ready, Clay," he called, "I'll be setting in the house a while with that sweet little Caroline."

32

Clay grabbed the milk bucket and stood up. "Thanks for taking care of Betsy, Doc," he said. "What do we owe you?"

"Your family will never owe *me* anything," the doctor said firmly. His tired brown eyes looked straight into Clay's.

"After Mr. Brown passes on through, you come by the office now and then. You can watch what doctoring is like, you hear?"

Clay promised he'd think about it sometime. He hurried out to meet Seth.

"Let's just ride down to the Brazos River, partner." The Ranger led the way on his big buckskin.

"Sure," Clay said, relieved. The barrel of his father's gun was digging into Clay's leg. He could feel a black-and-blue spot forming where the powder horn bounced against his hip.

He stared at Seth. How could he ride that way? The Ranger carried three revolvers in his belt. The rifle in the saddle had to be rubbing against his leg. There was a big knife swinging from a belt loop. There were rope lariats tied to his saddle, too, and a blanket. And one saddlebag. And nothing else.

"Why all the guns?" Clay had to ask.

Seth grinned. "I need every one of them in the thick of the battle," he said. "Besides, you can lose your scalp in the time it takes to reload."

Clay tried not to think about scalps. Or scalping. "Where are you staying?" he asked finally.

"Anywhere and nowhere."

Clay thought about that for a moment. "Well, then, where is the rest of your gear?"

"This is all a Ranger needs. I sleep on the saddle blanket. I've got an extra blanket along in case it's cold. Haven't needed that much, lately." Clay laughed. He could feel sweat trickling down his back inside his long johns.

"I use my saddle for a pillow and, in here," he patted his saddlebag, "I carry a pot for cooking, salt for seasoning, and a book for company."

"So where do you eat?"

"Out. Under the stars if I have to, in homes when I can." Clay thought of Seth sitting at his table yesterday for dinner. And, later, for supper. And Seth eating leftover biscuits with molasses and Caroline's best jam this morning.

Mama had refused to come out to sit with them and listen to more of Seth's stories. "I've heard enough," she had said.

"You see, Clay." Seth slowed his horse down to a walk. "We've got to travel light. Rangers are like rattlesnakes, sliding silently down a trail, striking out of nowhere, and leaving justice and peace behind."

Clay thought there was something wrong with that picture. "Justice and peace" from a snake? But Seth suddenly spurred his buckskin down the trail. Diamond was struggling to keep up. They cantered to the Brazos River before Clay had a chance to ask about the rattlesnake idea.

Seth got down from his horse near the muddy brown water. "Let's see what you can do," he said. "We'll use that stump across the river as a target."

Seth whipped one of the revolvers out of his belt, popped a cap onto the first cylinder's cone, and fired five times. From this close, the muzzle flash was fiery red and as long as Clay's hand. The heavy *boom!* of each black powder explosion echoed up the river bottom and back down again. Smoke hung in the hot, still air.

Clay squinted at the log across the river. There were five hits, as far as he could see.

"Look at me," Seth said. Clay stared at the Ranger. "Now look at where we're shooting."

"Why?" Was this a trick?

"Just do it." Clay squinted hard to focus across the river again. "How many times did I hit that log?" Seth asked.

"Five, I think. It was a five-shot revolver, right?"

"Yes. A Paterson Colt, like yours. Now, see if you can see how many times I hit the tree trunk beside the log."

Clay stared hard across the river as Seth shot off another gun. One—he counted the blasts to himself—two, three, four, five, six. SIX?

"That gun fired six times!"

"Yes, I know. But how many times did I hit the log?" Thick smoke hung around them.

"No gun holds six rounds. How did you do that?"

"Oh, this is the new Walker Colt. You've never seen one?" Seth handed the revolver to Clay. "Some of the Rangers going to Mexico have them." No wonder Seth wasn't impressed with Pa's gun. Clay felt stupid for a moment.

"What's this?" He pointed to a slender rod under the barrel of the new Colt.

"I'll show you. First, load your Paterson." Clay took the loading lever off his neck and pulled five balls from the ammunition pouch. He counted out five caps and closed the primer tin carefully. He used the bottom of the lever to pry off the muzzle so he could get to the cylinder. His fingers felt clumsy with Seth watching.

One chamber at a time, he measured the gunpowder in. He forced the balls down on top. Then he set a cap on the back of each chamber. At last he could close up the gun. He put the loading lever back around his neck. "Ready," he said.

"Not bad," said Seth. Clay knew he was lying. "But imagine trying to do all that on horseback."

"You can't. You'd drop a piece of the gun."

"Not a Colt." Seth reloaded six rounds of powder, balls, and caps into the new-style revolver. Clay watched in amazement.

"You don't have to take the gun apart!" he finally gasped.

"I can fire, reload, and fire again without having to get off the horse."

Clay was speechless, trying to imagine what it would mean to fight that way on horseback.

"Now, try firing your own gun at that stump."

Clay cocked his revolver and the trigger swung into place. He handled the gun like a fistful of spiny cactus while he tried to aim it. He wished the old Paterson had a guard over the trigger the way Seth's Colt did. It would be so much safer.

Clay squinted across the river and shot off the five rounds he'd loaded. He didn't think he'd hit the log once. He couldn't tell. "How'd I do?" he asked.

"You need spectacles."

"What?"

"You're squinting when you look far away because you need eyeglasses." Clay felt as if he'd been shot in the gut. "You mean I can't kill a Comanche?"

"Almost all gunfights take place face-to-face. That's the way it is. And you wouldn't have any trouble shooting from that close. But you might have trouble with the government."

"I thought Rangers could shoot Indians anywhere in Texas."

"We're not living under Texas law now. United States laws are different when it comes to Indians. But it won't matter anyway."

"Why?"

"All the Comanches will be gone soon anyway!" Seth grinned and winked. "At least they will if I have anything to say about it."

Comanches!

"Yah-hoo!" A scream came from upriver. Hoofbeats pounded toward Clay and Seth. "Ki-yai-yiiiii!" It was an Indian war cry—but it was a young boy's voice. Clay knew the voice. "Relax, Seth, it's just the MacMurtry boys, trying to scare us," he said.

"You sure?" Seth had both of his Patersons drawn and cocked. The horses charged into view, each carrying two or three boys whooping and snickering. Another horse carried a stranger with a huge blond beard and mustache.

"Well, there's nothing wrong with your hearing, partner." Seth lowered the hammers carefully and put the guns back into his belt.

The boys pulled their horses up and jumped off. "Howdy, Seth," the stranger said. "Ready to go?"

Seth's grin was as wide as Clay had ever seen it. "Clay, I'd like you to meet Jim Boyle, the meanest sidewinder they ever let into the Texas Rangers. We're about to take a little ride into Mexico again."

Jim took off his hat and swept into a courtly bow. A Mexican silver sword clanked at his side, and the maple stocks of two rifles stood ready in his saddle.

"We going to get paid this time?" Seth asked Jim. "They still owe me 37 dollars for the last month I rode with them."

"You know it doesn't matter to me. I always get paid one way or another." Jim drew the sword and waved it over his head.

Seth laughed. "Sometimes I think you'd pay the Rangers for the chance to fight!"

"I'll pay! How much does it cost?" asked Sam, the middle MacMurtry. Seth and Jim laughed all the louder.

"What about patrolling for Indian war parties?" Clay asked. "Aren't you supposed to be doing that?"

"All the time," Seth said.

"The way I see it, Clay," Jim added, "there's room in this here Republic for every Indian: the Comanches, the Kiowas, the Wacos, the Wichitas, and all the others. They're all welcome here—dead, scalped, and in their graves."

The MacMurtry boys whooped and started to dance, Indian style. Jim drew two revolvers from his belt and pretended to shoot them, one at a time. They lay on the

ground moaning and giggling, jerking and gasping until all were still. Then Jim swung both guns toward Clay.

"This isn't a game!" Clay said evenly. When he looked up from the revolvers into Jim's eyes, Clay felt a sickness in the back of his throat. The Ranger's eyes were the color of a snake's when it's just about to shed: blue-white and icy cold. And Clay knew better than to fool with a snake in the blue. He held his breath. He heard the clicks of guns being cocked.

"Shoot him, shoot him!" little Tommy MacMurtry called from the ground.

Seth stepped between Clay and the guns. "This isn't a game for Jim, either," he said quietly. "He's the craziest Ranger I ever met. But I guess he's earned the right to be this way. He lost family to the Cherokee years ago."

I lost family too, Clay wanted to say, but the memory of Jim's cold eyes kept him silent. A terrible thought shot through his mind. Do my eyes look like that? Do they? He felt his shoulders sag.

"Aw, I wouldn't hurt a pup like him!" Jim roared. "You know that, Seth. Now get your back out of my way. We've got Indians to chase."

"Yah-hoo!" Robert MacMurtry yelled. "And we're going along!"

"What's this?" Seth asked.

"We were out scouting along the stream bottom yesterday," the oldest MacMurtry said. "We came across an Indian camp. A warrior and his people are all there, just waiting to attack!"

"He's all painted up for war, too, and his hair is full of feathers," said little Tommy. "I saw him."

"Did they see you?" Seth asked quickly.

"N-no."

"Tell me how many braves there were, exactly."

"Well, one. But he looked mean. And he had a horse," Bart Mansfield said. Clay was surprised that Bart was running with the MacMurtrys and the rest. He didn't seem the kind to gang up. "And there was a nasty Indian child with him too."

"If they had a horse, Seth, we'd better be after them." Jim was swinging up into the saddle. "I got a pretty good idea of where to go looking along the stream."

"You think they're telling the truth?" Seth asked. "There haven't been Indians in this close for more than a month, far as I've heard tell."

"They're there," Clay said suddenly. "I heard them in the wash where I saw the bull." He remembered the cries. "One of them might be hurt."

"Then time's a-wasting," Jim said. Seth mounted up. He turned toward the boys before spurring his horse away from the river. "This just became official Ranger business. I don't want you boys following along, you hear?" And they were gone.

"Did you see them too?" Robert asked. He didn't wait for an answer. "Looked like that little one was hurt bad."

"Let's go watch, Robert," Bart begged. "That first Ranger said we could."

"Yeah. I want to see me some shooting!" The

MacMurtrys all laughed as Tommy pulled out a stick and pretended to shoot, then pretended again to be shot.

"Seth said to stay away," Clay warned.

"Well, he's *your* friend. *Our* Ranger said 'Come on and watch the fun.' "

"This will be great," another MacMurtry said as they climbed onto the horses. "Let's go get 'em!"

"You coming?" they called back to Clay, but nobody waited to hear his answer.

Clay stood alone by the riverbank and watched the Brazos River slip by. He didn't want to be there. He wanted to ride out and see what was happening. He picked up a flat stone and skipped it across the water. He picked up a fistful of flat stones.

"Official Ranger business," Seth had said. That made it all the better. Clay was going to *be* a Ranger someday. He should know what official business was like. And Robert had said the little one was hurt bad. Maybe I could help, Clay thought, like I did with Betsy.

He skipped another stone. Seth didn't want boys along, but he might be glad to see Doc Williams. "Come by the office anytime." Clay remembered the warm look in Doc's eyes when he had said that. Doc really meant it. And if he asked Clay to ride along, well, that would be just fine, too.

Clay dropped the rest of the stones. "Diamond," he told his horse as he mounted up. "We've got to get the Doc!"

Warriors

"Oh, Clayton, I'm so glad you're here!" Clay didn't stop pushing the pump handle. The ride had left him thirsty, and he had another dusty ride ahead. "Mama's out of Dr. Jake's medicine and the peddler isn't due into town for a couple of weeks."

"I'm on my way to Doc Williams's office, Caroline. I'm on official Ranger business. I don't have time to stop."

"Mama's half wild with pain already. Maybe Doc Williams has something . . ."

"And maybe Mama could try to live without it." Clay gulped cold water from the dipper and poured the rest on his head. What he'd said about Mama was as shocking as the icy water running down his neck—and it felt just as good.

"Seth said he's going to take me away from this, Clay. And he said he'll take care of you, too. And Betsy."

"Oh, Caro." Clay didn't know where to begin. "I . . ."

"I'm going with him, Clay. I just want you to know."

"I'll ask the doctor what to do about Mama," he promised as he swung into Diamond's saddle.

"You say they need me?" Doc Williams asked.

"Well, I don't know that for a fact. But there was a child hurt. And it looked like there was going to be some shooting."

"There generally is around Jack's boys when they're fixing to go off on the warpath."

"What?"

"Some of those Rangers don't have the sense you and I do, that's all."

Clay thought about Jim's eyes. "But we need the Rangers!"

"That we do. And you need to see what Rangering is all about, don't you? Saddle up my horse for me. I'll pack my bag in case there's anybody left I can still help."

Hurry, Clayton kept thinking. Hurry. But the doctor held his horse to a slow trot all the way to the stream.

"Now, where exactly are these warriors supposed to be?" Doc asked.

Clay thought about which way the shouts had come

from. And which way the bull had gone. "Right over that bank, or a bit upstream. There was a longhorn holed up down there."

"Get out your gun, then, son. You're aching for a reason to use it."

Clay took out a cap and primed the first shot in his Paterson. "Ready," he said, and they headed over the bank.

The smell of gunpowder hung in the still air of the wash. Clay and Doc Williams walked their horses slowly upstream. Clay held his breath, listening for the sounds of hooves over the babble of the stream. He didn't know whether to expect the hoofbeats of an angry bull or of charging war ponies. What he heard instead was choking.

Around the bend they came across the younger MacMurtrys. Two were still on horseback. Bart was throwing up into the bushes. "What happened?" Clay asked.

"Did you see the bull?" Doc Williams asked.

"Dead," said Tommy. "All dead." He looked like he might throw up too.

"Go home," Doc said to the boys. Bart wiped his mouth on his sleeve and nodded. There were tears in his eyes. Throwing up was the only reason his own eyes ever got watery, Clay remembered. Well, almost the only reason.

"Put the gun away, Clay," the doctor said. "It doesn't seem you'll need it."

They found the bull around the next bend. It was lying on its side with two arrows sticking out of its neck. Someone had started to butcher it where it fell. Most of the skin had been peeled off and great strips of meat had been cut out. There was blood on the ground. There was blood in the stream, too. And more blood was coming from upstream.

Clay looked up the wash. "You don't need to do this, Clay," Doc Williams said. The mockingbird started singing from his perch. Clay took a breath and squeezed Diamond's sides gently.

The Indians lay around the next bend. There were two. Clay got off his horse in silence and stared. His mind went numb as he tried to make sense of what he was seeing.

The child was a girl. She was little, like Betsy. She had bloody cloths tied on her arm and leg. Where those bandages had pulled off, her skin was ripped. Inside it was glisteny and smooth. Fat and muscle and tendons. Like Betsy.

But she'd been shot.

The Indian man lying beyond her had been shot too. And he'd been scalped. Blood still oozed from the wound on his head. A fierce longing swept over Clay. Papa had looked like this. Clay ran forward, then stopped.

Papa *hadn't* looked like this, his mind argued. Papa was young and strong. And dead. And scalped. And a Comanche had done it.

This man was old. Under the blood, his face was

wrinkled; the flesh on his arms was loose. He was a Comanche, but he was old. And dead. And scalped. Who could have done it?

Clay's mind went blank and empty.

Doc Williams's warm hand settled on his shoulder. "Seen enough?" he asked gently. Clay nodded.

"We'll send somebody out to bury them," Doc said. He led Clay back to the horses.

As they rode away, Clay's thoughts echoed the *clop-clopping* of the horses' hooves. Never shoot first. Never give up. Never give in.

Then one last thought flooded his mind. Take no prisoners. No prisoners. None.

They were halfway home before Clay could trust his voice. "I wanted to do that," he said quietly. "I wanted to make the Comanches pay for what they did to my family."

The Rangers were mounting their horses in front of the house when Clay and Doc Williams pulled up. Jim's sword glittered in the afternoon sun. "Looks like we didn't need your help after all, Doc," Seth said.

"And we won't be needing it anymore," Jim said. "We're heading south to join Major Hays. We're going to kill us some Mexicans!" Jim added. His eyes were glittering just like his sword, Clay thought.

Seth spread his mouth in that big, friendly grin. "Like I told that pretty little sister of yours, Clay, I just might be back."

"Who scalped him?" Clay asked.

"What?" Seth asked.

"Who scalped him?"

Seth and Jim looked at each other. Jim shrugged. "Guess I did. He deserved it. He was just another murdering Comanche." The horses shifted nervously.

"Well, *adiós*, partner!" Seth finally said.

Both Rangers had their horses spurred to a full gallop before they'd left the yard.

"You want me to come in?" Doc Williams asked. Clay shook his head no. He felt tired everywhere, tired all through. Tired and empty.

"Remember what I said, now. You can drop by the office anytime. Spend a few years helping me and you could take up doctoring yourself, you know. You think about it, you hear?"

And Clay did.

ABOUT THIS BOOK

Those early Texas Rangers were a special kind of man. They had to be, for they were sworn to defend a land soaked in violence. The Republic of Texas was huge, wild, and rugged, its climate harsh, and farming nearly impossible. Yet three groups loved it enough to fight—and die—for it.

The Native Americans were there first, of course. It was their land, but it was not a peaceful one. Tribes raided other tribes for horses, land, and power. Attacks and counterattacks followed as tribes tried to get even with one another.

English-speaking settlers wrongly called the natives "Indians." They battled these "Indians" and the Spanish-speaking settlers. As hurt built upon hurt, wars raged. Some wars were fought by governments and armies, tribes and war parties. Others were fought by individual people out for revenge. Those who wanted to live quiet lives— Natives, Texans, or Mexicans—were helpless.

In 1823, when the area was still part of Mexico, Stephen Austin was in charge of keeping the peace in the English-speaking colony of Austin. He got permission to hire ten men to "range and guard the frontier" against raids by Native Americans. This was the very beginning of the Texas Rangers—although the men weren't called Rangers and Texas wasn't even a state yet!

In 1835, Texans fought for freedom from Mexico. They paid men to range far and wide to defend against the Natives while they fought the Mexicans. By 1836, the president of the new Republic of Texas, Sam Houston, had organized 280 "mounted riflemen in the ranging service of the frontier." Not until 1838 were they officially called Rangers. When Texas became the United States of America's 28th state, in 1845, the Rangers were still needed to fight for law and order.

In the early days, Rangers handed out their own justice. Later they arrested criminals and brought them to jails, where they would be held for trial. Some of the men joined the Rangers to help keep the peace. Others joined for the thrill of action and adventure. They all had to be full of courage to wander the vast state, never knowing what sort of trouble they would be facing. They had to be good with a horse—and with a gun.

Today's Rangers are no longer a fighting force. Instead they are special police officers, serving under the Texas Department of Public Safety. Only men—and women since 1972—who have proved their bravery through years of service in law enforcement are invited to wear the Lone Star pin of the Texas Ranger.

K.V.K.